I0784063

The Adventures of
Guppie and Meep
by Rachel Hurbon

MILTON & HUGO L.L.C.
4407 Park Ave., Suite 5
Union City, NJ 07087, USA

Website: www. miltonandhugo.com
Hotline: 1- 888-778-0033
Email: info@miltonandhugo.com

Ordering Information:
Quantity sales. Special discounts are available on quantity purchases by corporations, associations, and others. For details, contact the publisher at the address above.

Library of Congress Control Number: 2025918441
ISBN-13:   979-8-89285-664-5   [Paperback Edition]
                979-8-89285-666-9   [Hardback Edition]
                979-8-89285-665-2   [Digital Edition]

Rev. date: 08/14/2025

The Adventures of Guppie and Meep

by Rachel Hurbon

If you go into the woods, you'll
find a pond more or less

Though a bog would be better to call it I guess.

In this pond you'll find a little green frog,

And he lives in the water underneath a wet log.

His name is Guppie and his best friend is Meep,

A swan that is graceful and white as a sheep.

Guppie met Meep late in the night,

When Meep brought Guppie a jar of firefly light

These two had been friends for now, quite a while,

This pond where they laughed,
talked, swam and had smiled.

When the sun rose that day they
decided to go on a picnic.

Near the pond was a berry bush, Meep
lifted Guppie, who picked it.

They then took the berries and made blueberry pie,

And they sat on the grass looking up at the sky.

When the finished their picnic, at around 12:10,

They made more pies to bring to their friends.

The first stop they made was to their friend Shawn,

Who in front of his house was a quaint little lawn.

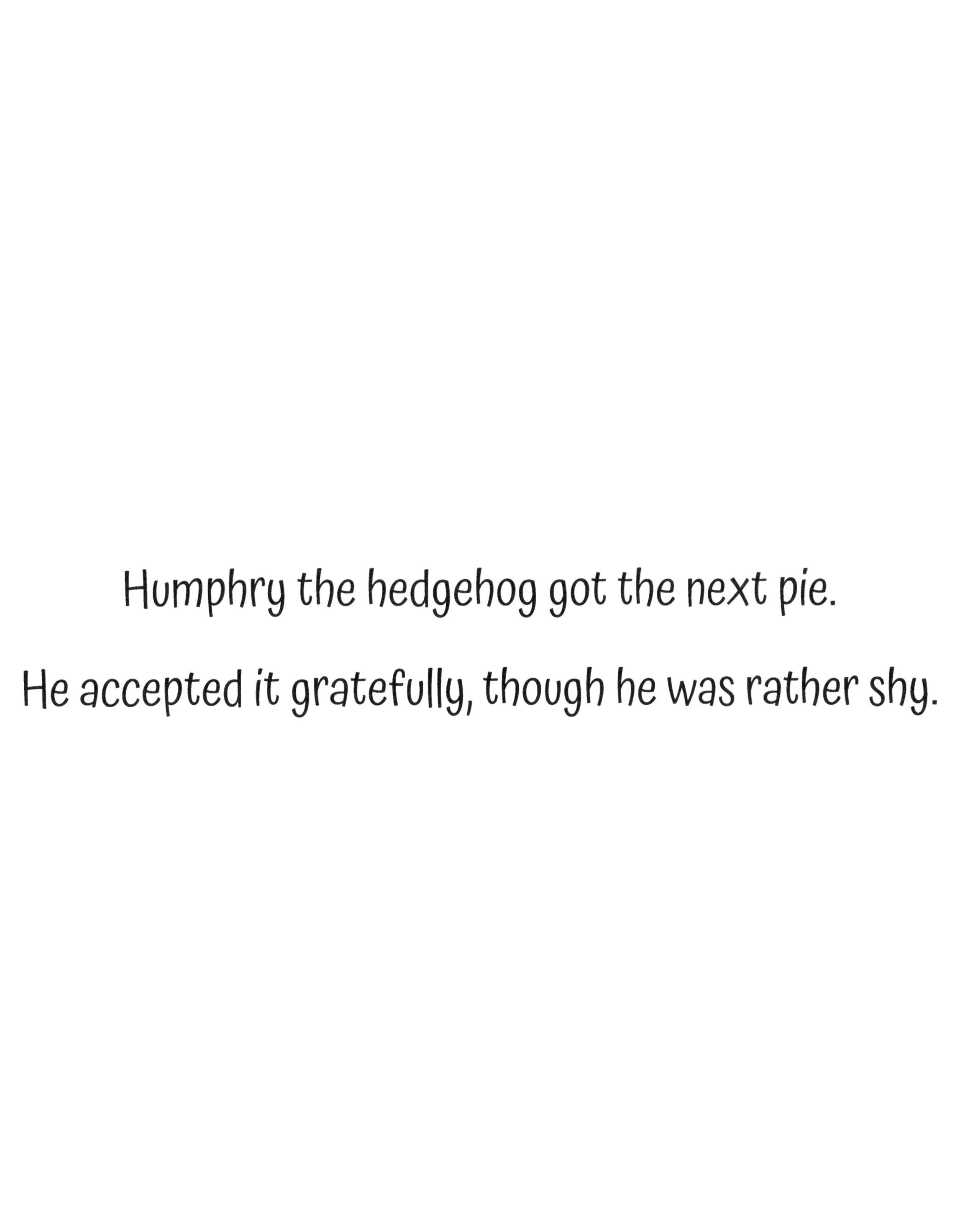

Humphry the hedgehog got the next pie.

He accepted it gratefully, though he was rather shy.

The last stop of the day was a burrow in the hill

And this friend, though not large,
had many sharp quills.

Porqué was his name and he loved blueberry pie.

When he received his gift he
hugged it and let out a sigh.

With the pies now all gone, Meep
and Guppie went home.

Guppie was tired so Meep had just flown.

They got back to the pond at the
first glimpse of starlight.

Once again in the water they
settled down for the night.

Guppie, still tired, fell right to sleep

And slept through the night under
the watchful eye of Meep